SUPP...
EMPLOYEE OF THE YEAR

A painter, a driver, a copywriter, and even a chef, Suppandi has applied his truly unique logic to almost every imaginable job out there. The perpetual optimist, Suppandi is never afraid to take up a new occupation, much to the amusement of his fans everywhere. Suppandi has remained, from the day of the character's conception, *Tinkle*'s most popular toon.

Based on Tamil folklore, Suppandi was first drawn by the legendary Ram Waeerkar. His daughter, Archana Amberkar, took over after he passed away. She gave the character a more youthful look. In this collection, we have put together Suppandi tales illustrated by Archana Amberkar, Prachi Killekar, Vineet Nair and Abhijeet Kini.

Prachi Killekar has drawn several Little Suppandi episodes which showcase the childhood escapades of our hero. Suppandi has a resume that is long enough to fill an entire book. We came up with this Collection keeping that thought in mind—we hope you love it!

Even Charlie Chaplin cannot beat Suppandi!
— **Tirth,** *Chennai*

Suppandi's innocence makes me laugh till my stomach hurts.
— **Misha Sharma,** *New Delhi*

Suppandi is funny and promises to keep *Tinkle* readers smiling!
— **N. Vimala Darshani,** *Tamil Nadu.*

Suppandi's bizarre ideas provide me my regular dose of humor.
— **Shreya Shenoy,** *Mumbai.*

Suppandi is truly a treat!
— **M. Naufa,** *Tamil Nadu*

Suppandi stories are always a good laugh!
— **K. Helsa,** *Andhra Pradesh*

I love the way Suppandi thinks!
— **Azrin Nizam,** *Dammam, Kingdom of Saudi Arabia*

SUPPANDI HANDS UP!

Story & Script
Dolly Pahlajani

Pencils & Inks
Archana Amberkar

Colours
Umesh Sarode

Letters
Pranay Bendre

AND LET'S DO IT ONCE MORE!

A-1-2-3—

3—EEEEEEEEEE!

WHAT HAPPENED, SUPP? ARE YOU OKAY?

I CAN'T MOVE, FROOTY! IT HURTS!

OH DEAR, I THINK YOU MUST HAVE PULLED A MUSCLE. YOU SHOULD GO HOME AND REST. BATHE WITH WARM WATER.

BUT... I'LL MISS THE REST OF THE WORKOUT.

DON'T WORRY, I'LL TEACH YOU LATER. GO HOME NOW.

UH... FROOTY... HOW DO I OPEN THE DOOR? MY HANDS SIMPLY WON'T MOVE.

OH, DON'T LOOK SO GLUM, JUST USE YOUR BUM! HEHEHEHE!

BONK

WOW! WHY DIDN'T MY BUM THINK OF THAT?

SOON...

AT LEAST TRAVELLING IN THE LOCAL TRAIN IS EASIER WITH MY HANDS UP.

WHOEVER PUT THE HANDLES UP THERE MUST HAVE PULLED HIS MUSCLES TOO.

HEY, YOU.

WOULD YOU LIKE TO SIT FOR A BIT? YOU LOOK LIKE YOU COULD USE SOME REST.

ER... ARE YOU GETTING OFF AT THE NEXT STATION, MA'AM?

DEAR ME, NO! I CAN'T GET OFF UNTIL I FIND WHAT I'M LOOKING FOR. YOU SIT DOWN FOR A BIT.

OH, THANK YOU, MA'AM. I WOULD HAVE HELPED YOU FIND WHAT YOU WANT, BUT MY HANDS ARE STUCK. I PULLED A MUSCLE, YOU KNOW.

AHHHHH! THANK YOU. PERHAPS I DID NEED TO SIT DOWN.

AND I DID NEED TO MAKE YOU SIT DOWN.

BECAUSE YOU'RE KIND?

NO. BECAUSE YOU ARE PREY! EHE!

B-BUT, I'M NOT PREY. MY NAME'S SUPPANDI! AND I THINK MY BUM'S STUCK TO THIS SEAT!

I'VE BEEN OFFERING SEATS TO PEOPLE ALL WEEK IN THE HOPE OF FINDING A PURE-HEART. THE SEAT CHOSE YOU. AND NOW I CAN COOK AND EAT YOU.

EAT? SURELY, YOU MEAN 'MEET'?

OH, YES, MEAT. I'VE BEEN HUNGRY FOR FAR TOO LONG! LET'S GO!

HEHEHAHAHAHA!

HEY! WHY THE CLOAK? I'M NOT FEELING—

—COLD.

HERE WE ARE!

WHERE'S 'HERE'? WHERE DID THE TRAIN GO?

IT WENT ON ITS WAY, JUST LIKE YOU WILL NOW.

HUP TO IT!

OW! WHY ARE YOU POKING ME, MA'AM??

TO GET YOU GOING. I'M FAMISHED! MOVE IT!

NOW, MY OVEN IS ALREADY WARMED UP. LIE DOWN ON THIS.

OH, THIS IS LIKE A SPA TREATMENT, ISN'T IT? MADDY HAD IT LAST WEEK! HE SAID IT WAS LIKE AN OVEN IN THERE. WHAT A SURPRISE!

YOU REALLY ARE KIND. THIS SPA WILL LOOSEN UP MY MUSCLES AND MAKE ME FEEL BETTER, WON'T IT?

IT WILL, IF YOU FIT INTO THE SPACE. PUT YOUR ARMS DOWN, BOY.

B-BUT, I CAN'T. BUT I REALLY WANT THE SPA TREATMENT. WILL YOU HELP ME TAKE THEM DOWN?

OF COURSE, I WILL.

WHAT COOPERATIVE PREY!

UHHHHH. PULL YOUR ARMS DOWN! UFFFFF!

I'M TRYING, MA'AM. IT HURTS! OWWW!

NO! I'M NOT RESTING UNTIL YOU FIT INTO—

OH!

AAA!

OW! I'M TOO OLD FOR THIS!

THUMP!

6

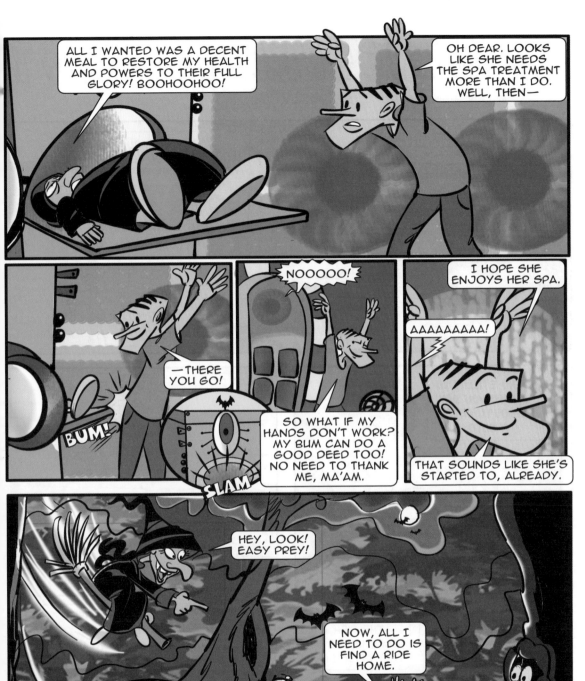

ONCE WHEN SUPPANDI WAS YOUNG 1

STORY: MRINALINI   ART: PRACHI KILLEKAR   COLOUR: SHAILEE

THIS IS FUN!

THAT'S ENOUGH, LITTLE SUPPANDI. YOU'VE PLAYED ENOUGH IN THE WATER!

STAND STILL! I'VE TO WIPE YOU DRY OR YOU'LL CATCH A COLD!

AWWW....MUM!

NEXT DAY-

???

WHAT ARE YOU DOING, LITTLE SUPPANDI?!!!

THE FISH HAVE BEEN IN THE WATER THE WHOLE DAY, MOM!

I'M WIPING THEM SO THEY DON'T CATCH COLD!

SUPPANDI: POLISHED

Story	Script	Pencils & Inks	Colours	Letters
Sanjitha V.	Sean Sequeira	Archana Amberkar	Umesh Sarode	Prasad Sawant

EXCUSE ME, SIR. WHY ARE YOU SCRUBBING YOUR SHOES?

I AM NOT SCRUBBING THEM, SUPPANDI. I AM POLISHING THEM WITH SHOE POLISH. IT MAKES THEM SHINY!

THE NEXT DAY—

SUPPANDI, THIS T-SHIRT IS DIRTY. PLEASE WASH IT WELL. I WANT IT TO BE BRIGHT AND SHINY AGAIN.

OKAY, SIR.

A FEW HOURS LATER—

SUPPANDI! WHAT HAVE YOU DONE? YOU'VE MADE MY T-SHIRT DIRTIER THAN BEFORE!

NO, SIR. I AM DOING AS YOU INSTRUCTED. YOU WANTED THE T-SHIRT TO BE SHINY SO I'M POLISHING IT—JUST LIKE YOUR SHOES!

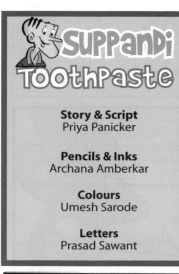

SUPPANDI TOOTHPASTE

Story & Script
Priya Panicker

Pencils & Inks
Archana Amberkar

Colours
Umesh Sarode

Letters
Prasad Sawant

ONE MORNING—

UH-OH! IT'S 9 A.M. ALREADY! I HAVE TO BE AT WORK IN 30 MINUTES.

YIKES! I'M OUT OF TOOTHPASTE! SUPPANDI!

WHAT'S UP, MADDY?

SUPPANDI, CAN YOU PLEASE RUN DOWN TO THE CORNER SHOP AND GET ME SOME TOOTHPASTE QUICKLY?

AFTER A VERY LONG TIME—

SUPPANDI, WHERE WERE YOU AND WHERE IS MY TOOTHPASTE?

I COULDN'T FIND ONE, MADDY.

THE ONLY TOOTHPASTE THEY HAD WAS FOR BAD BREATH AND TOOTH DECAY. AND YOU ALREADY HAVE BOTH, SO I DIDN'T GET IT!

smack

UGH!

10

SUPPANDI: A WAY TO SPACE

Concept	**Script**	**Pencils & Inks**	**Colours**	**Letters**
Chandni Shah	Aparna Sundaresan	Archana Amberkar	Umesh Sarode	Prasad Sawant

SUPPANDI: *The Genius*

Writer
Archita Mitra

Pencils & Inks
Archana Amberkar

Colours
Pragati Agrawal

Letters
Pranay Bendre

SUPPANDI'S EMPLOYER, A VERY CLEVER MAN, WAS THROWING A PARTY FOR HIS FRIENDS—

I AM THE CLEVEREST MAN ON EARTH! MY NAME IS IN THE HUINESS BOOK OF RECORDS. I CHALLENGE ANYONE HERE TO ASK ME A QUESTION THAT I CAN'T ANSWER!

WHAT IS 2,50,495 MULTIPLIED BY 1,10,797?

27,754,094,515.

WHO BUILT THE FIRST PYRAMID IN EGYPT?

PHARAOH DJOSER AND HIS ROYAL ARCHITECT IMHOTEP. ANY MORE QUESTIONS?

I HAVE A QUESTION, SIR. HOW MANY BRICKS DO YOU NEED TO FINISH A SEVEN-STOREY BUILDING?

WHAT? I... I... HMM... UMM... UH...

I–I DON'T KNOW! HOW MANY DO YOU NEED?

ONE! YOU NEED JUST ONE BRICK TO FINISH THE BUILDING!

ONCE WHEN SUPPANDI WAS YOUNG 2

STORY: SUJATHA MENON ART: PRACHI KILLEKAR COLOUR: SHAILEE

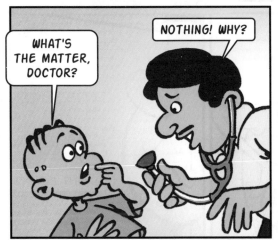

SUPPANDI
THE CURE FOR STOMACH ACHE

Story	Script	Pencils & Inks	Colours	Letters
Eesha Bhargava	Sean Sequeira	Archana Amberkar	Pragati Agrawal	Pranay Bendre

ONE DAY—

OOER... OW!

SUPPANDI, YOU CAN'T WORK WITH A STOMACH ACHE! GO TO A DOCTOR. FOLLOW THEIR INSTRUCTIONS AND GET BETTER.

UH! YES, SIR.

A COUPLE OF DAYS LATER—

UMM... SUPPANDI, WHAT ARE YOU DOING?

OH, SIR, I AM JUST FOLLOWING THE DOCTOR'S INSTRUCTIONS TO FIX MY STOMACH ACHE.

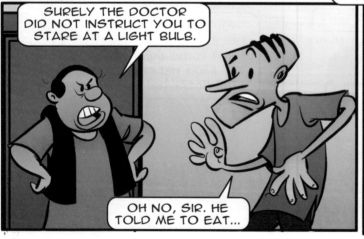

SURELY THE DOCTOR DID NOT INSTRUCT YOU TO STARE AT A LIGHT BULB.

OH NO, SIR. HE TOLD ME TO EAT...

MUNCH MUNCH

...LIGHT FOOD.

ARGH!

14

SUPPANDI Order's Up

Story
T. S. Karthik

Script
Shruti Dave

Pencils & Inks
Archana Amberkar

Colours
Umesh Sarode

Letters
Pranay Bendre

SUPPANDI: Basket Case

Based on an oral tale

Script	**Pencils & Inks**	**Colours**	**Letters**
Aparna Sundaresan	Vineet Nair	Umesh Sarode	Pranay Bendre

SUPPANDI WAS VISITING HIS GRANDMOTHER DURING THE SUMMER. ONE DAY—

THE VILLAGE SARPANCH HAS ASKED TO MEET ME TO DISCUSS AN IMPORTANT MATTER. HE WANTS MY WISE COUNSEL, HE SAYS!

THIS IS SUCH AN HONOUR, SUPPANDI. HE'S A VERY IMPORTANT AND CLEVER MAN. YOU'LL LEARN A THING OR TWO FROM HIM. YOU MUST COME ALONG.

OF COURSE!

WITHIN MINUTES—

ALL DRESSED? GOOD! I'LL JUST PACK OUR LUNCH AND WE'LL BE OFF.

GRANNY, THAT BASKET IS TOO OLD. IT WON'T LOOK GOOD IN FRONT OF THE SARPANCH

YOU'RE RIGHT, SUPPANDI. WHAT SHOULD WE DO?

HERE, USE MY BASKET. IT'S NEW.

AND SO THEY SET OFF. ON THE WAY, THEY BUMPED INTO SOMEONE—

SUPPANDI, THIS IS DR. VAIDYANATHAN, THE VILLAGE PHYSICIAN. DOCTOR, THIS IS MY GRANDSON, SUPPANDI.

PLEASED TO MEET YOU, YOUNG MAN. WHERE ARE YOU TWO OFF TO?

THE SARPANCH HAS CALLED GRANNY FOR AN IMPORTANT MEETING. DOESN'T SHE LOOK IMPRESSIVE? AND THIS BASKET IS ALSO IMPRESSIVE, ISN'T IT? IT'S **MINE**.

EH?

DON'T SAY THE BASKET IS YOURS, SUPPANDI! IT'S EMBARRASSING AND MAKES ME LOOK SILLY.

YES, GRANNY.

SOON, THEY BUMPED INTO ANOTHER IMPORTANT PERSON—

MR. MALAMAAL, MEET MY GRANDSON, SUPPANDI. SUPPANDI, MR. MALAMAAL IS THE VILLAGE BANKER.

GOOD MORNING, SIR!

GOOD MORNING, SUPPANDI. LOOKING AROUND THE VILLAGE?

NO. THE SARPANCH HAS CALLED GRANNY FOR AN IMPORTANT MEETING. DOESN'T SHE LOOK IMPRESSIVE? AND THIS IMPRESSIVE BASKET... UMM... IT'S **HERS**!

WHAT?

18

SUPPANDI: A WANTED MAN

Writer
Aparna Sundaresan

Pencils & Inks
Vineet Nair

Colours
Pragati Agrawal

Letters
Pranay Bendre

I'D LIKE TO APPLY FOR THE JOB, SIR! I DON'T HAVE ANY EXPERIENCE, BUT I'M SURE I'LL DO WELL.

WHAT JOB? WE DON'T HAVE ANY VACANCIES.

THEN WHY DID YOU POST ADS ALL OVER THE CITY?

EH? WHAT AD ARE YOU TALKING ABOUT?

THIS ONE. YOU SAY A TALL AND THIN MAN IS WANTED FOR A THEFT IN BADEE SQUARE. I'M TALL AND THIN! HIRE ME AND LET ME BE THAT MAN!

WANTED

ULP!

SUPPANDI
SECRET TO HEALTH

Writer
Archita Mitra

Pencils & Inks
Archana Amberkar

Colours
Umesh Sarode

Letters
Pranay Bendre

SUPPANDI WAS WORKING FOR A NUTRITIONIST—

WHY ARE YOU POURING COLOURED WATER ON THE PLANTS, SIR?

IT'S WATER WITH NUTRIENTS. THE PLANTS WILL ABSORB THE NUTRIENTS, STAY HEALTHY AND GROW TALL.

LATER THAT MORNING—

I DON'T LIKE MILK! I WON'T DRINK IT!

YOU HAVE TO DRINK MILK. IT HAS NUTRIENTS WHICH WILL HELP YOU GROW TALL AND STRONG.

I HAVE AN IDEA!

SUPPANDI! WHY ARE YOU POURING MILK ON MY SON?!?

...HE WILL AT LEAST ABSORB THE NUTRIENTS AND GROW TALL.

DON'T WORRY, SIR. IF YOUR SON WON'T DRINK THE MILK...

GRR!

SUPPANDI: No Harm Done

Writer
Sean Sequeira

Pencils & Inks
Vineet Nair

Colours
Pragati Agrawal

Letters
Pranay Bendre

SUPPANDI WAS WORKING FOR A ROGUE MILKMAN—

I HAVE TO DILUTE THE MILK TO INCREASE MY STOCK AND SALES. BUT IT'S OKAY. IT'S JUST A LITTLE BIT OF WATER. IT'S NOT GOING TO DO ANY HARM.

I'M LEAVING YOU WITH THIS PAIL OF FRESH MILK. ADD WATER TO IT AND TURN IT INTO TWO PAILS—BUT MAKE SURE IT STAYS WHITE!

OKAY, SIR!

A FEW MINUTES LATER—

SUPPANDI, WHAT ARE YOU DOING?! WHY ARE YOU POURING WHITE PAINT INTO THE MILK?

SIR, I FOLLOWED YOUR INSTRUCTIONS AND POURED WATER INTO THE MILK.

BUT I ADDED TOO MUCH AND THE WHITE COLOUR FADED, SO I HAD TO ADD SOME WHITE COLOUR. BUT IT'S OKAY...

White Paint

IT'S JUST A LITTLE BIT OF PAINT. IT'S NOT GOING TO DO ANY HARM.

GAH!

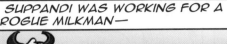

21

USEFUL VEGETABLE

ART: ARCHANA AMBERKAR
COLOUR: SHAILEE

WHAT DAY IS IT, MADDY?

TUESDAY... OR IS IT...

...WAIT, I'LL TELL YOU FOR CERTAIN...

...BAINGAN! THAT MEANS IT'S WEDNESDAY! MOTHER ALWAYS GIVES ME BRINJAL FOR LUNCH ON WEDNESDAYS.

WEDNESDAY? THEN TODAY'S MY VEGETABLE BUYING DAY!

DO I SEE BRINJAL? EXCELLENT!

IT'S ONE OF MY FAVOURITE VEGETABLES! IT'S NOT ONLY TASTY, IT'S NUTRITIOUS TOO!

ANOTHER THING ABOUT BRINJAL, UNCLE...

...IT CAN ALSO TELL THE DAY OF THE WEEK!

?!!!

22

SUPPaNDi
Critical Wife

Story
T. S. Karthik

Script
Sean Sequeira

Pencils & Inks
Archana Amberkar

Colours
Pragati Agrawal

Letters
Pranay Bendre

SUPPANDI HAD RECENTLY BECOME AN ASSISTANT IN A HOSPITAL—

YOU WILL PICK UP THE WORK QUICKLY. JUST REMEMBER TO HELP EVERY PATIENT AND NEVER REFUSE ANYONE MEDICAL ATTENTION, ESPECIALLY IF THEY ARE CRITICAL.

THE NEXT DAY, THE DOCTOR'S ANGRY WIFE WAS VISITING THE HOSPITAL—

YOU ARE ALWAYS IN THE HOSPITAL—NEVER AT HOME. WHO IS GOING TO HELP IN THE HOUSE? NOT YOU! WHAT GREAT WORK ARE YOU DOING HERE? HUH?

LATER—

I HATE WHEN MY WIFE VISITS ME IN THE HOSPITAL. SHE HAS NOTHING NICE TO SAY. SHE IS ALWAYS CRITICAL.

OH NO! THAT MUST BE WHY SHE IS SO ANGRY. I MUST HELP.

UNHAND ME, YOU RUFFIAN! **LET ME GO!**

I'M GOING TO HAVE TO CALL YOU BACK. THERE SEEMS TO BE SOME PROBLEM AT THE HOSPITAL.

SUPPANDI! WHAT ARE YOU DOING? LET GO OF MY WIFE!

SIR, I AM JUST FOLLOWING YOUR ORDERS.

WHAT DO YOU MEAN?

I HEARD YOU SAY YOUR WIFE IS CRITICAL. I WAS JUST TRYING TO GET HER MEDICAL HELP BEFORE SHE GETS WORSE!

Little Suppandi
Capital

Story & Script
Priya Panicker

Pencils & Inks
Archana Amberkar

Colours
Umesh Sarode

Letters
Pranay Bendre

IT'S ANOTHER FUN LEARNING DAY IN SCHOOL FOR LITTLE SUPPANDI.

OKAY, CLASS. TODAY WE WILL LEARN ABOUT COUNTRIES AND THEIR CAPITALS!

WHO CAN TELL ME WHAT THE CAPITAL OF THIS COUNTRY IS?

I, I!

YOU??!

NOT 'U', NEHA MA'AM. THE LETTER 'I' IS THE CAPITAL IN ITALY.

SUPPANDI: Washing Hair

Story	Script	Pencils & Inks	Colours	Letters
Pragun Pudukoli	Sean Sequeira	Archana Amberkar	Pragati Agrawal	Pranay Bendre

SUPPANDI WAS WORKING FOR A RICH FARMER WHO WAS VERY FOND OF ANIMALS—

SUPPANDI, STOP PLOUGHING THE FIELD. COME HERE.

YES, SIR, HOW CAN I HELP?

YOU'VE DESTROYED ALL THE CROPS. I'M GOING TO GIVE YOU SOMETHING SIMPLE TO DO. SOMETHING YOU CAN'T GET WRONG.

OKAY, SIR. I'M VERY EXCITED! WHAT DO I DO FIRST?

I'M ESPECIALLY FOND OF MY LOVELY HARE AND IT'S GOTTEN QUITE DIRTY. PLEASE WASH MY HARE FIRST.

OKAY, SIR. GOT IT!

BUT THEN—

SUPPANDI, YOU FOOL! WHAT ARE YOU DOING?

SPLASH

SIR, PLEASE STAND STILL. I'M TRYING TO WASH YOUR HAIR!

AAAH! SUPPANDI! NOT MY HAIR— MY HARE!

Little Suppandi — BACK TO SCHOOL

Story Elias Hussain **Script** Sean D'mello **Pencils & Inks** Archana Amberkar **Colourist** Umesh Sarode **Letters** Pranay Bendre

UNCLE, WHY ARE YOU STICKING THE LETTER 'L' ON YOUR CAR?

OH, HELLO, SUPPANDI. I'M DOING IT BECAUSE MY DAUGHTER IS GOING TO LEARN DRIVING FROM TOMORROW.

IF I STICK THIS LETTER, EVERYONE WILL BE MORE PATIENT WITH HER.

HMMM...

THE NEXT MORNING—

SUPPANDI, YOU'D BETTER HURRY UP. IT'S YOUR FIRST DAY AT SCHOOL TODAY.

MUM, WHY DO I HAVE TO GO TO SCHOOL?

SO THAT YOU CAN STUDY DIFFERENT SUBJECTS AND LEARN THINGS. NOW ARE YOU READY TO GO?

NOT YET, MUM. THERE'S SOMETHING I NEED TO DO!

MINUTES LATER—

SUPPANDI! WHAT HAVE YOU DONE TO YOUR UNIFORM?

OH, THAT...

...IT'S SO THAT EVERYONE KNOWS I'M LEARNING AND IS PATIENT WITH ME.

26

Little Suppandi
Big Maths Problem

Story
T.S. Karthik

Script
Sean Sequeira

Pencils & Inks
Archana Amberkar

Colours
Pragati Agrawal

Letters
Pranay Bendre

LITTLE SUPPANDI WAS STUDYING MATHS—

OKAY, STUDENTS. YOU KNOW THE BASICS NOW, SO TELL ME—IF THERE ARE 20 SHEEP IN A ROOM AND I CHASE FOUR OUT, HOW MANY SHEEP WILL REMAIN?

15!

17!

16!

ZERO.

HUH? SUPPANDI, HOW CAN YOU SAY **ZERO**?

IF YOU SUBTRACT FOUR FROM 20, THE ANSWER IS **16**. SEEMS LIKE YOU HAVEN'T LEARNT ANYTHING OF ADDITION AND SUBTRACTION!

BUT IF YOU CHASE FOUR SHEEP OUT OF THE ROOM, ALL THE OTHERS WOULD FOLLOW THEM. SEEMS LIKE YOU HAVEN'T HEARD OF HERD MENTALITY, TEACHER!

SUPPandi

Perks

Writer
Archita Mitra

Pencils & Inks
Archana Amberkar

Colours
Umesh Sarode

Letters
Pranay Bendre

SUPPANDI WAS BEING INTERVIEWED FOR A NEW JOB—

THE COMPANY WILL GIVE YOU FOUR WEEKS' LEAVE EVERY YEAR.

ONLY FOUR WEEKS? THAT'S NOT A LOT. I WOULD GET EIGHT WEEKS IN MY LAST OFFICE.

REALLY? OKAY, THEN. APART FROM YOUR SALARY YOU WILL GET TWO FESTIVE BONUSES!

JUST TWO? MY LAST WORKPLACE GAVE ME A QUARTERLY BONUS, FOUR FESTIVE BONUSES AND A CAKE AT CHRISTMAS PLUS, I WAS ALLOWED TO TAKE HOME ALL THE STATIONERY. I EVEN GOT FREE FOOD WHENEVER I WANTED!

THAT SOUNDS TOO GOOD TO BE TRUE! WHY DID YOU LEAVE?

(SIGH) THE COMPANY WENT BANKRUPT.

ENOUGH ABOUT ME NOW. LET'S TAKE A BREAK AND DISCOVER SOME OF THE OTHER STARS OF THE *TINKLE* WORLD.

MEET FRIENDS OF SUPPANDI

Ina Mina Mynah Mo:

Meet my friends Ina, Mina, Mynah, and Mo. The fabulous four who drive their father, Jagannath, up the wall! The eldest, Ina, is a fashion freak. Mina is forever confused. Mynah loves books and Mo is a foodie! Like my employers they are constantly full of demands which drive their miserly father crazy! But their father's constant

efforts to get out of spending usually backfire—just like my efforts to ease my employers' woes! Much to the girls' and their mother's delight, he always ends up paying up anyway—wonder when Jaggy will learn! Join them in all the fun they have as they try to figure out their lives and find their own paths—hopefully they won't have to change a lot of jobs before they get it right! 😄

Dental Diaries:

Meet my unfortunate buddy, Billy, the fangless vampire. His sole aim in life is to get his own set of fully-functioning fangs so he can suck blood from humans—does it mean he wants to be a mosquito? 😄 Well… the good thing is that his overprotective and highly affectionate mother is always by his side. Just like Maddy helps me find new jobs, Billy's mother helps him in his quest to get new fangs. The bad thing is that the world of the undead is full of terrifying monsters, ghouls, zombies, and more—all of whom are out to get Billy. Yikes! Billy's mission

to find fangs is often ruined by the dangerous vampire hunter Van HelSingh. Myra Vamptop—both his object of affection and his nemesis—also adds to his heart's (and tooth's) troubles by stopping him at every turn from getting those new fangs. Indeed, Billy's life is more of a misadventure than mine!

HEHEHEHEHE! IT TICKLES! HEE!

SIGH!

AWESOME ACTING, MISTER! YOU HAD ME GOING FOR A MINUTE... SUCH A NATURAL!

I'M A HUGE FAN OF THE VAMPIRE CULT. CAN I HAVE A LOOK AT THOSE FANGS? THEY LOOKED SO REAL...

SURE, WHATEVER.

WELL, THEY'RE KIND OF BOUNCY...

WELL, YES... IT'S A BIRTH DEFECT. CAN'T KEEP THEM OUT FOR TOO LONG.

BIRTH DEFECT? C'MON THEY'RE NOT REAL...

WHATEVER YOU SAY.

BLIMEY!

POOF!

33

HE'S THE 29TH, BUT HE MIGHT JUST BE THE ONE TO HELP OUR BILLY.

HERE, DEARIE, HAVE YOUR DINNER AND THEN WE'LL GO.

THIS SHALL BE MY LAST STRAW-AND-BOTTLE DINNER! SOON, I'LL BE ABLE TO...

...GAK! MO...OM, TOO... TIGHT...

OH, SORRY, DEARIE...

SOON—

READY?

YES, MA.

KEEP MR. CHUCKLES BACK. YOU'RE A GROWN MAN NOW, BILLY.

(SIGH) DOESN'T MEAN I DON'T NEED COMFORTING.

BYE, MR. CHUCKLES.

POOF! POOF!

34

HERE WE ARE!

POP!

TING TONG!

POP!

DR. GRIMM?

YES?

I'M MRS. DRAIN AND THIS IS MY SON, BILLY. HE HAS UMM... A DENTAL ISSUE.

MADAM, MY CONSULTING HOURS ARE LONG OVER. PLEASE VISIT MY CLINIC TOMORROW.

I WOULD, BUT THERE'S A MINOR PROBLEM...

OH! WELL, WHY DIDN'T YOU SAY SO? COME IN, COME IN.

WOW! YOU'RE NOT SCARED A BIT.

AT MY AGE, YOUNG MAN, YOU'VE SEEN IT ALL. COME RIGHT IN. WHAT SEEMS TO BE THE PROBLEM?

THIS.

OH... HMMM. THIS MAY TAKE A WHILE.

BOING! BOING!

35

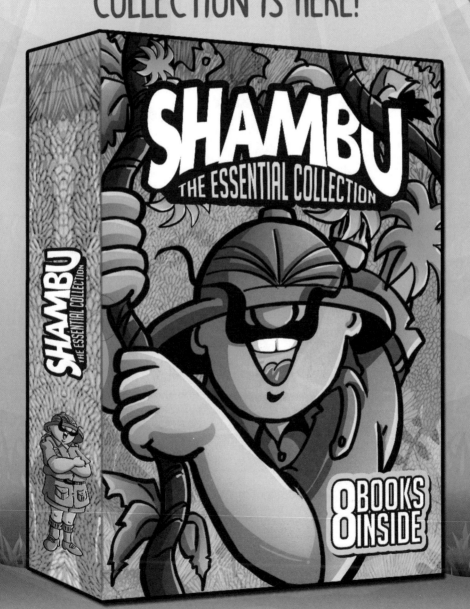

INA, MINA, MYNAH, MO
IN
TICKETS!

Writer: Rajani Thindiath
Illustrator: Archana Amberkar
Colourist: Umesh Sarode

WHERE ARE YOU OFF TO?

I'VE TO SEE ABOUT TICKETS FOR OUR ANNUAL VISIT TO...

TIMBUKTOO!

TO OUR ROOTS, INA! TO OUR ANCESTRAL HOUSE. THE ONLY HOUSE IN THE VILLAGE WITH TWO STOREYS AND RUNNING WATER...

...AND LEAKING ROOF AND OUTHOUSES!

WELL, OF COURSE! THAT'S THE JOY OF COUNTRY LIVING!

I'D RATHER GO TO **ANOTHER** COUNTRY!

YES, DAD! LET'S GO TO EGYPT OR CHINA...

ITALY, ROME, PARIS...!

SORRY, CHILDREN. BUT I'VE NOT WON A LOTTERY LATELY!

LET'S TRAVEL BY AIR THIS TIME!

BY AIR! THAT'LL TORPEDO THE ENTIRE VACATION BUDGET! **NO WAY**!

THEN AT LEAST BOOK AC TICKETS! IT GETS TOO HOT IN THE GENERAL COMPARTMENT!

AC! THAT'S **TWICE** THE COST OF A GENERAL TICKET!

COME ON, DAD! DON'T BE SO STINGY!

THE LAST TIME THERE WERE RATS...

...AND COCKROACHES...

...THE WASHROOMS WERE FILTHY!

ALL RIGHT! ALL RIGHT! I'LL GET AC TICKETS! SATISFIED?

YES!

THE NEXT DAY —

YES! YES! YES!

WHAT'S HAPPENED?

YOUR DAD'S NOT BEEN HIMSELF SINCE HE BOUGHT THOSE AC TICKETS!

BINA! LOOK! THEY'RE LAUNCHING THE *JANATA CHARIOT*!

WHAT'S THAT?

IT'S A NEW TRAIN! IT'S FULLY AIR-CONDITIONED AND...

...IT'S HALF THE PRICE OF OTHER AC TRAINS!

WOW! WHEN'S IT LAUNCHING, DAD?

THAT'S THE BEAUTY OF IT! IT FITS RIGHT IN WITH OUR PLANS...I'LL TELL THE BOOKING AGENT TO BOOK US ON THIS TRAIN!

NOTHING LIKE SAVING A FEW RUPEES TO PUT THE SPRING BACK IN HIS WALK!

AT THE BOOKING OFFICE —

I WANT TO CANCEL THE EARLIER BOOKING...

...AND BOOK SEATS ON THE JANATA CHARIOT? I'VE HAD A LOT OF CANCELLATIONS SINCE THE NEWS BROKE!

BUT YOU'LL HAVE TO PAY THE CANCELLATION CHARGES...

OH, THAT'S ALL RIGHT!

I STILL SAVE ABOUT... THREE THOUSAND RUPEES!

A FEW WEEKS LATER —

OH NO! OH NO! OH **NO**!

NOW WHAT?!

HOW **CAN** THEY DO THIS! THEY **CAN'T** DO THIS!

WHAT HAPPENED?

THE JANATA CHARIOT'S DEVELOPED SOME TECHNICAL SNAGS SO THEY'VE **POSTPONED** THE LAUNCH OF THE TRAIN!

NOW CALM DOWN... MAYBE YOU CAN...

43

YOU'RE RIGHT! I MUST CANCEL THOSE TICKETS!

BUT I DIDN'T SAY ANYTHING!

BOOK ME BACK ON THE EARLIER TRAIN!

I'M SORRY, SIR! THERE WAS A HUGE RUSH FOR THOSE TICKETS AFTER THE *JANATA CHARIOT'S* LAUNCH GOT POSTPONED! WE DON'T HAVE A **SINGLE** TICKET LEFT!

YOU DON'T EVEN HAVE **SIX** TICKETS?

WELL... IF YOU'RE WILLING TO PAY EXTRA... SIX TICKETS CAN BE ARRANGED!

HOW MUCH MORE?!

PSST... PSST...!

THAT'S TOO MUCH!

AS YOU WISH!

CROOKS! THEY THINK I'M HELPLESS!

WELL, I'LL JUST POSTPONE THE TRIP!

AT HOME —

POSTPONE THE HOLIDAY! ABSOLUTELY NOT!

BUT BINA...

45

SUPPANDi: Call Again Later

Writer
Archita Mitra

Pencils & Inks
Archana Amberkar

Colours
Umesh Sarode

Letters
Pranay Bendre

SUPPANDI WAS HELPING IN THE KITCHEN—

SUPPANDI, CALL MY SON AND TELL HIM TO BE HOME FOR DINNER BY 8 P.M. TODAY.

YES, MA'AM.

A FEW MINUTES LATER—

DID YOU CALL MY SON?

I CALLED HIM THRICE BUT EACH TIME A LADY ASKED ME TO CALL AGAIN.

THAT EVENING—

I TOLD YOU TO ANSWER ALL OUR CALLS! WHY DID YOU GIVE YOUR CELL PHONE TO SOME LADY?

I DIDN'T GIVE MY PHONE TO ANYONE! I WAS TALKING ON IT THE WHOLE DAY.

DON'T LIE TO ME! SUPPANDI SPOKE TO HER. SUPPANDI, TELL US WHAT THE LADY TOLD YOU OVER THE PHONE.

SHE KEPT SAYING, "THE NUMBER YOU ARE TRYING TO REACH IS CURRENTLY BUSY. PLEASE TRY AGAIN LATER. THANK YOU."

ACK!

SUPPANDI
What's up, Doc?

Story
T. S. Karthik

Script
Sean D'mello

Pencils & Inks
Archana Amberkar

Colours
Umesh Sarode

Letters
Pranay Bendre

WHAT'S THE MATTER?

DR. RAEED, I THINK I HAVE A SIMPLE ACIDITY OR INDIGESTION PROBLEM. IT CAN'T BE ANYTHING SERIOUS.

THANK YOU. BUT I'M THE DOCTOR. I KNOW BETTER.

NOW GO AND LIE DOWN. I'M GOING TO PRESS YOUR STOMACH. TELL ME IF YOU FEEL ANY PAIN.

OKAY.

DOES THIS HURT?

NO.

WHAT ABOUT NOW? ANY PAIN?

NO, DR. RAEED.

SO WHERE EXACTLY DOES IT HURT?

BUT YOU ARE THE DOCTOR. SHOULDN'T YOU KNOW BETTER?

AHHHH!

LITTLE SUPPANDI: Energy Saver

Story	**Script**	**Pencils & Inks**	**Colours**	**Letters**
Sajan Abraham	Sean Sequeira	Archana Amberkar	Umesh Sarode	Pranay Bendre

LITTLE SUPPANDI WAS IN HIS E.V.S. CLASS—

EVERYTHING WE DO USES ENERGY. THE MORE ENERGY WE USE, THE MORE WE DESTROY EARTH. WE SHOULD ALL TRY TO USE AS LITTLE ENERGY AS POSSIBLE.

(YAWN)

SECONDS LATER—

ZZZZ

SUPPANDI, WHY ARE YOU SLEEPING IN CLASS?

TAP TAP

MMM... I'M SAVING THE WORLD, MA'AM.

HUH? WHAT DO YOU MEAN?

YOU SAID WE SHOULD SAVE ENERGY. I USE VERY LITTLE ENERGY WHEN SLEEPING. AM I NOT SAVING THE PLANET?

HAHA HAHA HAHA

SUPPANDi's Vacation

Writer
Sean Sequeira

Pencils & Inks
Archana Amberkar

Colours
Umesh Sarode

Letters
Prasad Sawant

SUPPANDI WAS ON VACATION IN MEXICO—

I DON'T TAKE VACATIONS OFTEN, SO I'M A LITTLE CONFUSED. WHAT DO PEOPLE NORMALLY DO ON HOLIDAYS?

HOLIDAYS ARE ALL ABOUT HAVING FUN! WHAT DO YOU LIKE TO DO FOR FUN?

OH, NO-NO-NO-NO! THANK YOU! I FIND MEXICAN FOOD TOO SPICY. AND I'M NOT HUNGRY ANYWAY.

FUN? I DON'T KNOW. I LIKE TO WORK.

HA-HA! SEÑOR, WHY DON'T YOU TRY LEARNING SOMETHING NEW? WE HAVE A SALSA CLASS THIS AFTERNOON. IT MIGHT BE FUN!

SO NO SALSA, OR EVEN NACHOS FOR ME!

HUH?!

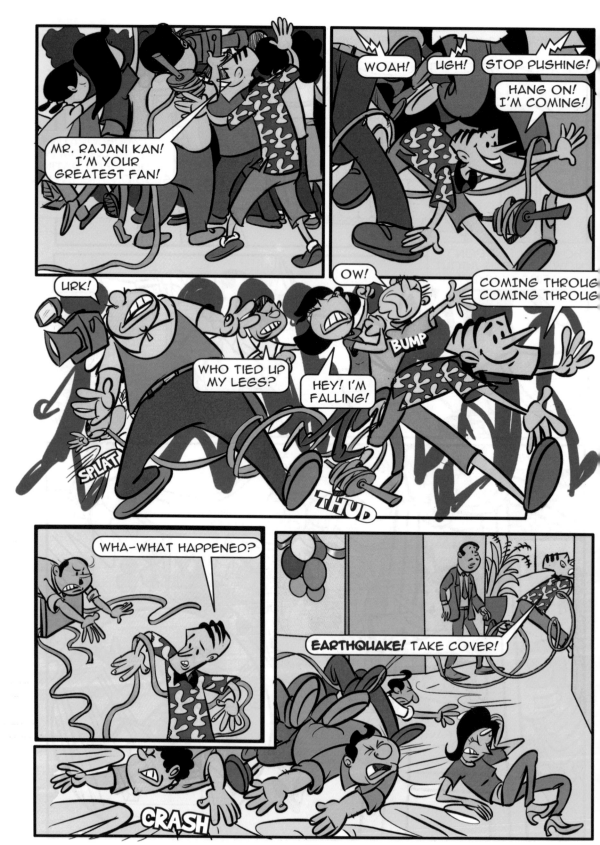

SUPPANDI: HELPFUL REMINDERS

Writer
Archita Mitra

Pencils & Inks
Vineet Nair

Colours
Umesh Sarode

Letters
Pranay Bendre

SUPPANDI'S EMPLOYER WAS GOING TO THE OFFICE—

SIR, YOU FORGOT YOUR—

PLOP

I AM IN A HURRY, SUPPANDI. JUST THROW IT DOWN.

OKAY! HERE'S YOUR BREAKFAST, SIR!

WHAT ON EARTH—

AND HERE'S YOUR JUICE TOO!

AND, SIR—

SPLASH

WAIT, SUPPANDI! DON'T THROW ANYTHING ELSE! I'M COMING UP TO GET IT!

YIIEEE!

A FEW MINUTES LATER—

WHAT NOW?

ACK!

YOU FORGOT YOUR TIE, SIR! BUT I DON'T THINK IT WILL MATCH WITH THE COLOURS ON YOUR SHIRT NOW.

SUPPANDI DRIVING DISASTER

Story & Script
Dolly Pahlajani

Pencils & Inks
Archana Amberkar

Colours
Umesh Sarode

Letters
Pranay Bendre

57

READ THROUGH THIS SPONSORSHIP LETTER AND CLEAN IT UP. DON'T FORGET TO SAVE IT... I'LL BE BACK IN SOME TIME.

YES, MA'AM.

HUH?

CLICK! CLICK!

AFTER TEN MINUTES—

SUPPANDI, WHY ARE YOU STARING AT A BLANK PAGE?

THIS IS THE SPONSORSHIP LETTER, MA'AM. I'VE CLEANED IT UP AND SAVED IT, JUST LIKE YOU'D ASKED ME TO.

WHAAT?!

HAHAHAHAHA!

LATER—

I CANNOT KEEP HIM HERE, MADDY. HE DELETED ALL THE TEXT FROM AN IMPORTANT FILE.

PLEASE GIVE HIM ANOTHER CHANCE, SIR! PLEASE?

(SIGH!) FINE. GO HELP THE LIBRARIAN. BUT REMEMBER—NO MORE MISTAKES!

I PROMISE, SIR!

BUT THIS TIME, THE MANAGER DECIDES TO WATCH SUPPANDI FROM A DISTANCE. SO, AT THE PARK—

WHY IS SUPPANDI MAKING US GO ROUND AND ROUND THE PARK?

NO IDEA. BUT I'M FEELING FAINT.

JUST SOME MORE TIME, AND WE'LL BE DONE.

SUPPANDI! WHAT ARE YOU DOING?

SIR, YOU ASKED ME TO TAKE THEM AROUND THE PARK FOR AN HOUR. I'VE DONE SO ONLY FOR 20 MINUTES NOW, BUT THEY'RE ALREADY DIZZY.

BUMP! BUMP!

SUPPANDI!!! LEAVE **NOW!**

AROUND THE PARK... HAHAHAHA!

HAAAHAHAHA... OH, DON'T FIRE HIM, MANAGER. HE HAS DONE WHAT NO ONE ELSE COULD.

WHAT'S THAT?

CAN'T YOU SEE? SUPPANDI HAS BROUGHT LAUGHTER BACK INTO OUR LIVES.

HAHAHA! TRUE. WE HAVEN'T LAUGHED LIKE THIS IN AGES.

!!

HE'S NO SuperBrain—

—BUT HE HAS A SuperHea

LOOKS LIKE SUPPANDI HAS FINALLY FOUND THE PERFECT JOB, OR HAS HE?

Suppandi's Magic Trick

Try this magic trick with ice to surprise your friends. Pour some water into a paper cup, mutter a few magic words, and when you empty the cup—hey, presto! Out falls an ice cube!

Before you start the trick:
● Get two similar, opaque cups. Your audience should think that you are using a single cup throughout the trick.
● Cut a cube of sponge that's large enough to fit snugly inside the cup. Stick it in the bottom of one of the cups and place an ice cube on it.
● Get hold of a box large enough to hold both cups.
● Place both cups inside the box—the special cup with the ice cube, and the empty cup.

Performing the trick:
● Show your friends the empty cup.
● Once they're convinced it's empty, tell them you'll turn it into a magic cup. Put it into the box, utter some magic words and pull out the special cup.
● Pour some water into the cup. As you pour, the sponge inside will start absorbing the water.
● Place your hand over the cup and mutter some more spells.
● When the sponge has absorbed all the water, tip the cup over and let the ice cube fall out. Tell your friends you have been given the magic touch of instant freezing!

Tips:
● Because ice melts quickly, prepare and perform the trick quickly.
● Use paper cups so you can crush and dispose them before your friends have the opportunity to perform an inspection!

Little Suppandi Makes a Friend

Writer
Aparna Sundaresan

Art
Abhijeet Kini Studios

Letters
Prasad Sawant

SUPPaNDi: Trial and Error

Writer
Archita Mitra

Pencils & Inks
Vineet Nair

Colours
Umesh Sarode

Letters
Pranay Bendre

SUPPANDI ACCOMPANIED HIS EMPLOYER TO A STATIONERY SHOP—

WHAT ARE YOU DOING, SIR?

I AM TESTING THIS PEN BEFORE BUYING IT. YOU MUST ALWAYS TEST SOMETHING BEFORE YOU PURCHASE IT, SUPPANDI, TO CHECK IF IT IS WORKING PROPERLY.

THAT EVENING—

AH, THIS TEA IS REALLY GOOD.

ULP! A POWER CUT! QUICK, SUPPANDI! GO LIGHT A CANDLE.

A FEW MINUTES LATER—

WHAT IS TAKING YOU SO LONG?

THIS MATCH WON'T LIGHT, SIR, AND I DON'T KNOW WHY.

IT WORKED PERFECTLY WHEN I TESTED IT IN THE SHOP!

ARGH!

SUPPANDI: Green Tea

Story	Script	Pencils & Inks	Colours	Letters
T. S. Karthik	Sean Sequeira	Archana Amberkar	Pragati Agrawal	Prasad Sawant

SUPPANDI HAD RECENTLY BECOME A BARISTA*—

ONE GREEN TEA, PLEASE.

CERTAINLY, SIR. PLEASE TAKE A SEAT.

HALF AN HOUR LATER—

WHAT'S GOING ON? IT'S BEEN HALF AN HOUR SINCE I ASKED FOR A CUP OF GREEN TEA!

ALMOST DONE, SIR.

HERE IT IS.

YUCK! WHAT'S THIS?

Food Colour

GREEN TEA—JUST LIKE YOU ASKED. THE TEA WAS READY 25 MINUTES AGO. I JUST HAD TO ADD THE COLOUR GREEN!

*A PERSON WHO WORKS IN A COFFEE SHOP

A CURE FOR ALL!

WRITER: ANISHA HARIHARAN | ART: ARCHANA AMBERKAR | COLOUR: SHAILEE

SUPPandi: Quick Repairs

Writer
Archita Mitra

Pencils & Inks
Archana Amberkar

Colours
Pragati Agrawal

Letters
Pranay Bendre

SUPPANDI WAS WORKING FOR AN ART COLLECTOR—

SMASH

OH NO!

DON'T WORRY, SUPPANDI! WE CAN REPAIR IT IN AN INSTANT.

A MINUTE LATER—

AS GOOD AS NEW! ALWAYS REMEMBER, THIS TUBE OF SUPERGLUE CAN REPAIR ANYTHING THAT BREAKS!

A WEEK LATER—

QUICK, SUPPANDI! GO FETCH THE DOCTOR! MY SON FELL AND BROKE HIS WRIST.

AAAH

I HAVE A BETTER IDEA, SIR.

WHY NOT USE THIS TUBE OF SUPERGLUE TO PUT IT BACK TOGETHER? IT CAN REPAIR ANYTHING THAT BREAKS, REMEMBER?

GAK!

HUH?!

Suppandi Bookish Blunders

Story & Script
Dolly Pahlajani

Pencils & Inks
Archana Amberkar

Colours
B. Meenakshi

Letters
Prasad Sawant

SO, SUPPANDI. YOU ARE THE NEW ASSISTANT?

YES, SIR.

GOOD-GOOD. START BY CLEANING UP BOOKS UNDER ALPHABET 'A'.

WHICH WAY, SIR?

THAT SIDE IS 'A'.

OH. THAT'S A LOT OF BOOKS, I WILL GET TO THEM RIGHT AWAY.

SPOOF

SPOOF

EEEEEE!

GRR.

SIR-SIR, THERE ARE BOOK WORMS IN THERE.

SHHHHH!

KEEP SILENCE, SUPPANDI. THIS IS A LIBRARY.

SORRY, SIR... BUT THOSE NASTY...